English text ©1997 Chronicle Books.
Illustrations ©1995 by L'Ecole des Loisirs.
All rights reserved.

Book design by Vandy Ritter.
Typeset in Electra and Regular Joe.
Printed in Hong Kong.

Library of Congress Cataloging-in-Publication Data available
ISBN: 0-8118-1640-0

Distributed in Canada by Raincoast Books
8680 Cambie Street, Vancouver, British Columbia V6P 6M9

10 9 8 7 6 5 4 3 2 1

Chronicle Books
85 Second Street, San Francisco, California 94105

Web Site: www.chronbooks.com

Papa!

by Philippe Corentin

chronicle books · san francisco

Late one night

in a warm bed

there was a noise.

Oh!?

Papa!

Papa! Papa! There's a monster in my bed!

Don't be afraid little one. Come with me.

What is it, honey? Did you have a bad dream?

Everything will be all right. There's no such thing as monsters.

There is nothing to be afraid of. It was just a dream.

Sweet dreams.

Oh!

Papa!

Papa! Papa! There's a monster in my bed.

Don't be afraid little one. Come with me.

What is it, honey? Did you have a bad dream?

Everything will be all right. There's no such thing as monsters.

There is nothing to be afraid of. It was just a dream.

Sweet dreams.

So, late at night

in a warm bed, remember...

there's no such thing as monsters.